THE

WHISKEY

POOL

GW00703020

When you look back and realise your whole life was lived on the edge.

A short story by

Dale Brendan Hyde (c)

Verso page

The Whiskey Pool ISBN: 978-1-912543-17-5

Published by Copyright(c) Dale Brendan Hyde. The right of Dale Brendan Hyde to be identified as the author of this work has been asserted by him in accordance with the copyright, designs and patents act, 1988

This is a work of fiction. Names, characters, businesses, places, events and incidents are either the products of the Authors imagination or used in a fictitious manner. Any resemblance to actual persons living or dead or actual events is purely coincidental.

Printed by Clays, elcograf S.p.A

THE AUTHOR ...

DALE BRENDAN HYDE was born in Salford in 1974 yet has lived most of his life in the City of Wakefield West Yorkshire.

A troubled life throughout his teens crescendo into a lengthy prison sentence for robbery, where upon release a mixture of attending college to retake failed schooling & continued trouble with the police & high courts seemed to be his course in life, until a university place seemingly became the catalyst to a more determined path of making his occupation that of a Writer.

He published his first poetry book by Route at the Yorkshire Art circus for the TS Elliot prize. Contributions to other writers books followed & magazine articles on his passion of bare knuckle boxing revealed his extensive repertoire in his writing styles.

Trouble free now for over a decade, his debut novel THE INK RUN finally showed the true depth of his talent.

His first short story, titled, The Whiskey Pool is available on Amazon kindle. He is currently over half way through his second crime fiction novel, Titled, The Death Row Thrift Shop, which will be released this winter 2018.

'What's in store for me, in the direction I don't take?' Kerouac.

'I drink to make other people more interesting' Hemingway.

'Being drunk is a good disguise. I drink so I can talk to assholes. This includes me' Jim Morrison.

'I only take a drink on two occasions- when I'm thirsty and when I'm not' Brendan Behan.

THE WHISKEY POOL

At some point, usually just after you have hit rock bottom, and when I say rock bottom, in this instance what I actually mean is slipping and falling from the summit of Everest and landing in to the colossus coal pile that the devil wants you to stoke for eternity in Hells fire bright.

Yes that rock bottom, well anyway just after you land there with a mighty thud, you have to remind yourself that everyone was doing their damn best for you and their selves in this game we call life. We all had our own mountain of personal problems, that some just learnt how to deal with much better than others. Some get all the way to the top and plant a flag to blow in the triumphant wind, while others fall to a messy death with only a pauper's grave to say they existed at all.

I don't fall into neither category, yet in all honesty fall into both, as I've had a successful life to a point and then also seen the gutter, as alcohol has been my rickety crutch throughout my whole adult life.

I was born with the moniker of Sean Seamus, but my friends, all three of them that are still rinsing on this mortal coil call me JJ. It stands for when I was a non-drinker out in the pubs swaying at the bar on the verge of falling off the wagon again, and they would say laughing," just juice?"... But I've been on the wagon for the previous two years now after twenty odd stood and sat supping away like there is no tomorrow, and that's really where this tale belongs, in the now, yet unfortunately like every wretched tale I will from time to time have to vault you back to a point where my reasons for becoming dry become obvious.

I'm on the edge right now, physically and mentally, as the battle rages from the moment my eyes peel like glue from my lids into the light of another day's reality. I hate myself in every conceivable way known possible to man. I'm a retch, a scoundrel, a misfit on a planet of what I consider morons. I can only just barely cope with a conversation if I was entirely out of my tiny mind on good knows what concoctions of booze, my staple diet mainly the dark brown demon of whiskey, but I'm sober and living in a worse hell than I'd ever known.

If anyone asked me if I thought there might have been a starting point for my terrible drinking spree, I guess in a joking manner I would always tell the tale about the flagon of cider that hit my Mothers head as my Father hit a brow of a hill at quite a speed in his

Morgan sports car, resulting in lift off and a rather heavy landing that catapulted this flagon of Cornish cider straight out of its resting place, which also happened to be the foot of my Moses basket and sailed through to the front colliding with the back of my Mother's bonce.

Naturally an almighty blaze of an argument broke out, even at that age it must have imprinted somewhat like the massive lump on my Mothers head. A rather scarred childhood of memories I'm afraid

I could recall with much effort the soft tickly sand beneath my infant toes as they had earlier in the day dangled me over the beaches beautiful sand, yet the lasting memory was the howl my Mother made as that cider flagon hit her and the screaming she hurled towards my Father, then the door slamming as he walked away, then the silence of pain left between me and Mother in the small confines of that majestic car.

Yes I'd say that's maybe where it all started. When you do something crazy and people jokingly say were you dropped as a baby, well funny they should mention that, as just before the cider flagon incident, before I'd popped out into the light of hope at my birth, my Mother had very late into her pregnancy actually dropped me as a nearly born child. A neighbour's dog on the rough council estate she had lived on before my Father came with his majestic ways and swept her away to the finer things in life, anyway a dog I recall my Grandmother saying was a German Shepherd had jumped up and knocked my Mother off balance, resulting in quite a heavy fall. Unfortunately I can't recall from inside the cocoon that disturbance, but a disturbance it must have been. My luck not much better as I'd just been born, maybe a couple of weeks old later and the damn same dog only went and jumped up again while Mother was cooing outside the house to the neighbour about my little black curls upon my head. This time she had managed to cushion rather courageously the fall, yet I had still slightly banged my head quite hard into the crook of her arm which she broke in two places in the effort to protect me. Again what I recall as a baby was the shadowy figure of my Grandfather flying out of the steps at the side of the house and letting off an almighty racket of a blast, which I found out much later was the shotgun going off both barrels into the dogs obliterated head.

Standing at the very edge of my indoor swimming pool I inched my toes closer to the very drop off point. The problem wasn't that I didn't know how to swim, nah the problem was I'd emptied the pool as soon as I'd bought the 17th century house and ever since I'd been using it to stop me from falling with a spectacular swoon right off the back tailgate of the fully stocked booze wagon and into its deep end. The fact that I'd never been able to swim and the horrid flashback of my father taking up the John Wayne approach to bringing up little boys, by way of throwing me into the old rag mills reservoir and watching me splutter and panic and bob under a few times before finally realising with irritation that he must dive in and save me from drowning to death had been the very reason for pulling the gigantic plug way back then after the cash purchase. Naturally like all street urchin kids who had only the becks n canals to jump in on hot summer days of youth, I'd craved the flamboyance of the rich estates and the certain houses we would peep over fences and as getting more braver, climbed to nosey in the windows of the ones who had luckily enough the pleasure of indoor swimming pools. So when my first novel got snapped up by the famous publishing house FULL CIRCLE, I'd been overjoyed to place that gutter kid stigma well and truly behind me and join the jet set swanning about like they didn't shit like normal folk. I stayed grounded though in the beginning, my Buddhist training as a young man serving me well as I grounded myself and held back the sniggers that were always only moments away from my face when I had to mingle on the celebrity scene of writers. The biggest bunch of pampered arses I'd ever encountered, with some of the industry movers and shakers only confirming to me at certain gatherings that jerks were well and truly in control of the business end of literature. Thankfully I'd not been some poor talented new comer having to cringe and arse lick these fools, as my debut had sailed up the charts and the money generated could not be ignored. I had clout thank god, in a world of untalented arrogant ink dippers.

But as the years rolled on, and the paunch in my gut swelled to where I'd not seen my cock for years I got pulled into the bullshit, air kissing cheeks that didn't care if you dropped dead on the spot. There were some fantastic people in the industry, don't get me wrong, with surprisingly some of the most powerful writers being rather sweet and giving with their time and encouragement to people rising up through the hard won ranks. But as I pointed out, my till ringing blessed me with having to not worry about making friends and influencing people, yet after four years at the top and my second novel following the stratosphere climb up the charts like my first, I caught the arse hole bug and started to think I was elevated above regular society. That's when it all came crashing down and my Buddhist teachings couldn't save me one jot. My third book crashed like a plane with two lost engines and I nose dived right off the bestseller radar, and oh boy how the vultures circled. I had stupidly believed that my first two successes guaranteed a third, putting aside the formula that had seen me land on my two feet amongst the elite. I'd become tired of following the herd who endlessly weighed down the book shop shelves with the same old tired looking covers and titles that didn't differ much from one book to the next. Where did my entire ink flowing heroes disappear to in the game? Where hid the mavericks who had put their soul into the page. Not these bores who churned out endless drivel as the publishers asked for, as the tills rang merrily away and played a tune of greed. As I have mentioned, my first two books had been great releases, as I'd followed the protocol and with a bitten lip and tongue, followed the remedy to get my books out there and flying off the shelves. The book I'd hand written and kept in my locked drawer of my davenport desk was the one that I had really wanted to unleash on the readers of this world's minds.

Crazily, after my two bestsellers, I thought they would be ready to hear from the real me, and how wrong I could ever have been. The publisher warned me and reluctantly because of the income I'd generated for a number of people involved in my first two, they had to follow my say so, and I had been strongly inclined to launch this third true novel, so out it went.

It sunk without trace into the black hole that was the charts. Outside the top ten, the top one hundred, the top ten thousand. It was dismal and so depressing, somewhere around a figure that was like reading back some long distance telephone digit.

I'd bombed, and the battle was over for me as I tried without vain to salvage via interviews and radio shows and the odd TV appearance some kind of second wind to go back to the ink well trenches. But it was to no avail and I retreated to my liquid brown demon friend and drunk myself mad.

These days looking back it must have been nearly twenty years since my name was in print. I'd become the legend inside of the public houses back then, amusing the bums as I joined them, there thinking irrational as to why I frequented their company, this Mr big of words and books. But over time they came to realise I was as lost as they and that the only real comfort lay at the bottom of a bottle.

You could zoom slowly forwards as like a repeat day started and ended, I put myself through the trip to echo springs and beyond. But time did keep moving and twenty hard years later I was finally sober, yet mentally drained of much of my clarity. The comeback was on I stupidly tried to convince myself within my head. I'd sharpen pencils and buy from online stationary stores new note books, promising myself I'd get back to winning ways. I would wander around the house blowing the deep inches of dust from the shelves of my bookcases where I'd in my youth been so fond of reading my inspirations of literature. I'd grab a copy of my own books that had bought the ruined empty shell of a home that I now stood in echoing around its lost love chambers, blowing n sneezing as I cleared the dust n read a few pages that had made me famous. It was still drivel to me and the anger would rise as to the ignorance of the masses who rarely knew when they had a genius in there dumb hands. I'd flick through the beauty of my third book, the flop, and wonder in astonishment at the foolishness of the sheeple who only wanted a book to get away from the dreariness of their lives for a few days. Not this grand effort of words structured to make you try to do nothing but god damn think about why the dreary life was still there when you closed those shallow books last pages.

I was a writer who held the qualities of the greats, yet I'd fallen on the dumb deaf ears of the world as it sheltered from some harsh realities, and only really cared for a story that you could see the ending a mile away. Where were the poetic lyrics these days and the risk takers? It was all money, money, money and I wanted nothing to do with its evil ways.

A quote from my youth tumbled back inside my brain and leapt out onto my tongue to say, 'A golden palace that is blood stained cannot be the abiding place for Buddha, A small hut where the moonlight leaks in through chinks in the roof can be transformed into a place where Buddha will abide, if the mind of its master is pure.'

I think up until last year all I'd done just before wobbling on the verge of downing a bottle of scotch was to empty the contents in what I thought was a rather triumphant way, spilling and splashing it into the deep end of the swimming pool. But that was last year, and I'd been alone now in this house for the last two.

Since this Christmas, I had started angrily smashing the whole contents into the blue and white tiled floor of the pool, giving the rather jagged and worrying look of something rather murky and dangerous awaiting my inevitable plunge into its rather quickly filling depths..

MY PALACE BLOOD STAINED FOR SURE.

When the wife left me a couple of years back to rattle around this ten bedroom home, I guess it wasn't too much of a surprise. The last real argument, yes the one that resulted in me hiding in the wild section of our three acre property, under a giant shrub, as I'd pulled in the early afternoon the cork yet again on another litre bottle of the brown liquid demon. Totally blottoed out, she had found me for the last time lazing on the blue flowery sofa semi-conscious muttering away to my little leprechaun pals. She had caught me mid flow into the conversation where I was telling them all about how this was definitely the last time and how I was about to pull myself together and finally shape up and be the man everyone knew and wanted me to be. Her rage had finally appeared this time and it was venomous, as she dragged me by the hair off the sofa while kicking me in the ribs with what for me was unluckily her most hardened pointy shoes. I guess the dog that I'd forgotten to walk, who was over on her favourite Persian rug busy chewing one of its fringed corners didn't help the scene she had walked in upon much either. His whiskers wet and whiskified as I'd kept dipping my fingers in the end of the bottle to pacify his whining to go out. Looking back it was for sure the straw that broke the proverbial camel's back for her.

She had packed light while smashing things upstairs while I had crawled on all fours out of the back of the utility room door and managed to rise into some stumbling resemblance of a walk like one of those Neanderthal t shirts showing monkey to man evolution and headed to the wild garden to think.

It had been here that we had our true last goodbye. Me upon my back rolling around on the floor while she stood over me with that frown that that aged her about thirty years and screamed at me to fuckin hurry up and die. I'd strangely only focused on the fact that she had packed my rather expensive LV holdall as the screaming that was flying spitting froth from her red lipstick lips went well and truly over my pissed head. I'd shouted incoherently at her vanishing back that wearing silk scarves around her neck didn't hide the fact that she was getting old, or something derogatory like that. Well who had paid for the plastic bitch in the first place, some young gigolo probably now going to get his filthy paws on those ten grand implants, but the surgeon after I'd had a quiet word in the posh corridors had informed me that no amount of money could hide the years of a sagging scrawny neck. A neck I knew she hated as I'd caught her so often sat in her boudoir dressing area lifting the skin up with her fingers on her cheek, pushing high into her ear area to the mirror pouting at its look, while I spied on her from the door left a jar, until she let it drop natural and I would disappear back down the landing.

That was the last I'd seen or heard from her since, except for the odd solicitor letter to sort out some split with the house contents and savings.

I had stuck to my word, the promise I'd made with my imaginary friends the day she had left though, forever, as I'd not let a drop touch my lips since. I was not prepared for the battle ahead though, as such a dirty war was raging internal inside me now I'd cracked up entirely since being left alone to fend for myself, with Alcohol being the most difficult of all addictions to get a grip and remain on good terms with as a sober man.

I remember when I came round from the slumber I'd drunkenly fallen into and managed to crawl back through the garden to the house in the falling light of the evening, to find her gone, and this time gone for good, which still shocks me to this very day as if a ghost of a shadow just sucked its familiar shape from besides me on my side and vanished leaving me with a blank pavement in the sun, my own shadow long gone from sight, drained entirely of any decent blood.

The Rolling Stones don't have nothing on me as I blasted away the silence of the large house with their hit record, nineteenth nervous breakdown, it was one of the many albums that I owned that luckily still played, as most were sticky with the bottle of cherry brandy I'd dropped over the crate I stored them in, on another mishap one night when I'd been slaughtered yet again. I'd play whiskey in the jar just to test my nerve as it had always been a rather grand drinking song to partner me along as I gulped from the bottle in the old days like the old book gunslinger I was.

But all that had been in the past, I'd done rather well considering I'd not seen my therapist for over a year now, the other reason being I just couldn't afford the extortionate fees and had been happy self-analysing my addiction. My three close friends who I joking referred to as Larry and the two Moe's didn't agree, ringing the house phone occasionally to inquire about my progress and balance and get the latest analysis on the truck\wagons role in my life . The actual truth was I'd told the shrink to stick his two hundred dollar an hour Yankee opinion up his own arse and that I would look back to the Buddhism of my youth to save me, to which on my last sighting of him, he had shaken a stern head in my direction warning me to not be foolish. My pride at not being able to cough up his fees easier to swerve in a rather grandiose gesture of, I know best, rather than admit I was stony broke. But Doctors in general were text book men, not out of the box natural thinkers when it came to all things healing. My Buddha would see me back onto the righteous path.

I had tried holding the incense of blue Lotus fragrance, burning it in my hand as the other clutched the familiar favourite bottled brand of brown liquid demon. The smoke that serenely drifted up towards my nostrils, no longer connecting me to the Buddhist paths of my youth, as smells more powerful coming off the rotting soggy labels engulfed my senses. The incense would be dropped into the mix with a fizzling plop and I'd be back focused on the supreme test that my brain was waging a war with. I couldn't allow myself to unscrew the top and take that fateful step back and drink from the demons neck. The smashing sound would always bring me back around though, enough at least to focus my bleary, sleepy eyes upon the ever expanding mess building up in the pools deep end. Some days I'd start the count again of the bottles that were visibly still somewhat intact, yet I never finished the count, slumping away in my now slouched over position to sulk in the dry sauna and massage uselessly at my temple headaches that were now constant.

I was forever on the edge of the pool more though now I'd done away with his services, always close to either diving in and ending the party for good or even more dangerous, biting off the top of a good bottle of the brown demon and going on one final drunken rampage where I pretty much knew I'd slay all those that had done me wrong over the years. My Buddhism and learning forgiveness and empathy going straight out of the window as soon as a drop touched my lips and my blood stream welcomed the demon, or just doing the right thing and hurling myself into what I termed the whiskey pool. I knew the correct term was a trip to echo springs, yet I'd broken my drinks cabinet in half with a wood axe quite some time ago, last Christmas Eve I believe to be exact.

Just one chug of the scorching liquid down my throat and I would be back to the maniac I always became while highly intoxicated. I didn't want to hurt anyone no more, especially my battle worn body and scar covered mind. No, the only thing to do was recall my more dangerous moments while I teetered on the edge and try to not fall either way, yet I knew there was going to be a point where a decision had to be made one way or the other.

I owed it to everyone who had given a flying fuck for my welfare over the years to at some point end this booze battle. The blue and white tiles that covered the floor to my indoor pool were becoming less distinct. The amount of broken glass and soggy labels combined with the dark fluid had given the floor to the pool a rather sinister ominous look. The title of my debut novel that I'd paid a small fortune to have inlaid in these imported tiles that had come out of an old abandoned monastery in Kerala now totally lost to the sloshing mess of liquid I was hurling in. It was like once these certain things disappeared so did even more so the logical parts of my sanity and reason.

I had been falling on and off the wagon for the past thirty plus years as a binge drinker. I guess that's the correct term these days.

I was a seasoned pro in the early years at hiding my addiction and a king at the sobering up game. I was also a complete fuckin loser, a lousy husband, a terrible friend and worst of all, my own worst enemy, and I was most formidable at the later too. Combined with my book writing fame, it was a terrible combination.

Only a month after she had gone for good I had stood on the edge of the indoor pool, my eyes serenely closed, clutching a large litre bottle in my left hand. The toes of my bare feet had been gripping the inner lip of the pool side, that's how close I was to falling in that time. I'd recalled the thoughts of all the injuries I'd occurred throughout my time as a booze clown. Just the incidents from the pubs and from leaving the watering holes of shame and heading home clinging to the very fabric of the walls of this ancient city I'm from.

All the goddamn scars were too real on my body. The broken hand that became mangled that way as I had fallen out of some rough public house doorway into the dim light of yet another wasted evening, my only sense of direction being the street lights just flickering on with that amber yellow glow. At a crossing a car screeched around the corner and some young punk had shouted from his open driver side window for me to move my pissed up bum away from the kerb edge. Mad as hell I'd run after the car as fast as I could while trying to focus with one bleary eye on the model and plate, all the while my brain sending messages to my mind hinting that I wished I could run faster than the car so as to be able to pull the fucking mouthy chav from his secure spot and kick his head to smithereens in the street. That's how the booze got me back then. The car had sped off and turned a corner out of sight and in my frustration I had lashed out a terrific ram rod punch at this concrete base of a lamp post, smashing away with a few good clouts until the pain momentarily sobered me up and made me wince and stop and mope off down the street cradling my hand like some limp dead child.

At the hospital five miles walk away I'd sobered right up and got the news after an X ray that not only was it badly broke but that the bone was twisted totally round inside the hand and I'd need emergency surgery right away. The next I remember after heading down flat on my back on a wobbling trolley that this rather jolly porter shoved with ease, was waking up on the ward with the hand wrapped like a mummy and my pal Larry sat stern and frowning in an orange plastic chair besides me. The grapes half eaten on his lap, which I straight away calculated, wondering if I ate enough would I get even the slightest wine kick from the juice.

That was quite mild though compared to the three nose breaks I had suffered, with the worse one needing my entire nose skin pulling away from the bone so they could chip away and clear the cartilage obstruction that held up my breathing like a strangle hold.

I guess the worse was my double fracture to the jaw, which was made even worse for the fact it turned out to be nothing at all to do with my behaviour and was just one of those unfortunate bumps into a total psychopath. You don't usual get two bumping into one another as its quite rare to get two real ones in the same shared vicinity, but that is how it played out, my bad fortune being I was in no fit state to retaliate as I'd been out drinking from around noon, slamming back Guinness pints with whiskey chasers poured into the white creamy froth, and it had been around three am the next day when the blow came. Stood swaying minding my own bizz I'd recalled up to a point thinking back that I had been on the verge of a taxi home from the city, lazily chewing over before jumping in one if I should either devour a kebab like a wild man or go for what I termed the more sophisticated pizza to munch slices on, then bang I was on my arse. Well not technically on my arse, but on to one knee, as this wally had come snaking through the small crowd without a word and socked me right to the left jaw.

If I'd have just gone properly down I'd have fared much better but I sprang at him from the knee I had taken to steady the impact and that's when he had caught me again with a sweet shot aimed downwards like a hurricane wind flying past my head and caved the other jaw side in. The old bill had seen the entire scene as I'd got up off my back and clutched my hand to my mouth, the sensation of a jaw break is something like all your teeth have fallen out and landed in the bottom palate of your mouth, very weird. The pigs realising I was just another drunken stumble bum ignored even ambling over to inquire and I was not likely walking down to complain so I made a rather feeble attempt to enter the club again where this wally had retreated to with the bouncer on the door now saying 'er lad do thi sen n me a favour n go get your sen up te ospitall', which I did, again after deciding to walk and sobering up with the wind giving my jaw a rather soft jittery shake. They had taken one look at me and I'd been on the trolley again for more surgery. The upshot of that one though was as soon as I was home and healing up, a week later my bloody wisdom tooth on the left bottom side decided to make an appearance. The infection that followed was agony as it could not get passed the metal plate inserted to hold the jaw, and after three days drinking and swilling neat whiskey around my teeth I'd had to go back in and have the plate out and tooth and then three weeks later back in again to have the plate re inserted.

I'd stewed for months on that one, getting a plan together with the two Moe's, which we tried to execute. On the corner near the bar he worked at, one Moe ran at a speed of a track star and delivered a beautiful professional heavy weighted punch to the temple of the doorman. With him sleeping soundly I'd pulled from my rucksack the milk bottle full of petrol and flicked the lighter to check all was in working order before walking briskly to the door to start my attack. The wally's brother came out to meet me as I was nearing the threshold pleading with me to leave it and promising me his brother was not working that night. I'd head-butted him in the nose breaking it nicely and glided past to scan the crowd. He wasn't there, fortunately for him, so I butted his brother on the way out again for good measure giving him a message to pass on that I would be back.

I think it was a month later that I noticed the wally's face in the local paper. He had been given twenty years for numerous naughty things, all violence, like breaking peoples legs with scaffolding bars and putting a clot on an old man's head like the soft arse bully he was. I turned the page and forgot it and put it down to another of my drunken stupid nights out.

But that was nothing compared to the wounds n hurt I'd dished out back over the years.

I'd burnt a good friend to death in the late eighties. I'd gotten away with the charge as it became clear no evidence of much clout to see me found guilty was available to the court and so I weaselled once more out of even the fairness of what should have been a manslaughter sentence. I had not intended to kill him in an inferno of the most wretched scorching melting flames, yet I'd been so inebriated I'd not done the slightest thing to help when any rational man would have.

What makes it worse was that this was not the first time I'd seen the flames as a killing tool. There had been another incident which I did fully intend on that occasion to murder in cold blood. A continuous Bad flashback occurred quite regular in my nightmares of when I'd rolled my old friend Reynolds over in his sleeping bag towards the one bar fire he had fallen asleep against in his bedsit dwelling. I callously turned the crank switch to raise the heat to its maximum three bars and waited until the edge of the bag caught light. I recalled sat in a nearby restaurant casually ordering Indian food and eating at a leisurely pace my korma until I calculated enough time would have passed to burn the sneaky no good treacherous bastard to death. I was that gone in my mind back then in those days, that I'd felt nothing but pure disappointment when instead of turning the corner back into Reynolds street and expecting a flurry of flashing lights from fire and ambulance, to finding a quiet eerier street and to walk back in the back door and finding him sat bolt upright at the back of the room hunched up on a work service, two lump hammers gripped tight in both hands , staring wild eyed yet still frightened at my appearance, his constant mumbling words trailing from his mouth, you tried to kill me, you tried to kill me, you tried to fuckin kill me, over and over and over again. I'd walked out without reply, disgusted in my wasted efforts to do away with him. Yeah that's how the liquid demon got me back then. Not a trace of my years of attempting to find Buddha's guidance, nor a jot of hope coming from a mind learned in the India ways, no I was nothing but a pure poisoned infected demon back then. It was flashbacks to my cruel coldness like this that kept the lids screwed on tight as I swayed on the edge of my indoor pool. It was also later the same flashbacks that caught me now smashing violently the bottles into the tiled floor instead of pouring.

With the dings ringing out into the silence of the pool gazebo where I'd planted on the old pool side bar the old royal to work away on, I had also secured in my own mind another great book deal, the one that was going to see me back on top of the charts. Long nights hitting the keys on the typewriter, punching out a rhythmic finger tipped gallop with fine speed that Kerouac would have nodded over an agreeable acknowledgment towards.

It staved off the cravings hitting the metal letters, yet after an hour or so I'd be hunting around my different stash areas for a bottle to caress in my hands, telling myself all the while that I would not take a sip and that it was always just a test. I suppose the caress of the curves of the fine shaped bottle had become my one and only true mistress.

Yet what fate awaits a man who fails, and how many rebirths was this? It was just another unanswered question that I knew no answer too. Yet I did know the whole point of trying my hardest not to drink again, where after internal struggle I'd managed after some horrid flashback to unscrew the cap and pour the rot away or much later when the remembering had become more detailed of my shenanigans, I had just done away with the pouring and straight smashed the glass vessel into the bottom of the tiled pool.

For the last month things had become intolerable though as I recalled incident after incident where the demon drink had spelled out most clear that it was my nemesis and not to be challenged.

I'd slept on a Lillo by the side of the sauna which had stopped steaming years ago. The thought of even trying to act normal and lay upstairs in bed was off putting to the extreme. In fact I very rarely ventured up the grand sweeping staircase to the many rooms the house retained, preferring to limit my roaming to the pool room or the kitchen or out into the wild part of the garden, although even the neat parts were wild now like my bodily hair that I'd stopped tending too many months ago.

The pure natural spring that weaved its way throughout my property, more or less as you stepped out of the back utility room door was like in a sense the only vein of health that connected itself back to me and surrounded me and reached out into some unknown part of nature. I'd sometimes years ago when I was really bad on the grog, have deep warm Jacuzzi baths upstairs in one of the many house bathrooms, the wife always appearing when I'd be on the verge of nodding off, her stern voice warnings about my imminent drowning, and she was probably right, but I didn't really care, but it wasn't like I was trying to kill myself then.

These days, a good year into my sobriety, I'd started crawling out of the back door, waking early. Again as a boozer and a writer I'd never really been one for the early cold mornings, usually waking around noon, but now on this new path of trying to see something good in myself and the world again I'd be up around six am. I'd crawl out of the back door as if on some kind of weird pilgrimage and I'd head a little way up towards the orchard and then lay myself down level with the grasses and reeds and watch some of the animals that are small that lived down there, which you tend to forget about but which have just as much right to their lives as ours even though they appear much more insignificant. They had as much going on in their own worlds which we shared.

I'd turned some rainbow rock small boulders onto their high sides and down level on the ground as it reminded me again of my Buddhist study days. It would stand and shine low in the back lit sunlight of the waking dawn, representing to me in moments of memory the great white snowy tipped summits of mountains I'd dared to climb as a young man, yet here on my beaten knees, I could only feel that inevitable avalanche a coming. The only real memory of those times when I felt close to figuring life out had been when I had rested after a hard mornings climbing upon a large boulder to rest the ache out of my calves after reaching the first great ledge. With my nail file that I'd flicked out from the side of my utility knife, I'd zoned out with the high altitude and started to remove some dirt from under my fingernails. After I got to my last left thumb to clean, I'd stared so intently at the small mound of Earth recovered from under the nail that it suddenly dawned upon me that my life and all of life and its sole existence rested just there. It was as simple as that.

After fascinating my vision I'd lean and cup my hands into the fresh cool waters. One splash, thank you God, two splashes, for the suffering of Jesus upon the cross, three splashes for the bodhisattvas, four and five in quick succession for the moon and the seas, and the sixth splash would get my sleepy tired eyes open and I'd say to myself, get up off your knees.

And I'd repeat this every morning, and it helped a little, but it never really stopped the bad thoughts coming back and by the noon

I'd be pool side, perilously close to the edge, always looking down at the whiskey bottle more or less glued to my hand.

I'd found the strength to keep on twisting the cap and pouring it away, but that was in the first year of sobriety but in this second year I'd started getting angry again and smashing the bottle hard into the pools floor, where it would shatter like my life's dreams and mix in soggy with the curling wet labels which started to look like thin lipped mouths laughing and mocking me. I was in a real mess, as I recall that later in the evening the dirty rain had dried upon the kitchen windows, from a distance looking out it looked like old parchment papers written with instructions on how I might get a grip. I didn't know if I Could find my way back onto the eight path fold, yet I'd been reading the scripts a long time as a young man, so it wasn't entirely out of reach and this was clearly a sign to me as I had been sat contemplating the flame as I stared into the flame of a bobbing candle on the kitchen worktop that I had started lighting again as the electric had cut out across the whole house now. The window looked as though someone had written straight across the glass, full stops and commas I could even see, yet upon nearing to investigate I realised in my tiredness it was just how the dirty rain had dried and streaked falling down in sheets against the glass, yet I still tried to take the message, but the black thought clouds soon came and swamped me again as the thunderous cloak wrapped around me like the nightmares I'd had of late.

The scoring system board had been the entry point, with points added and deducted by a faceless source. I knew in my dreams I would be reincarnated into the lower realms, although it might not appear so clear, but this is where the real tally would matter, where they will say well you did this, you did that, that wasn't very nice was it? As you scratch your head in wonderment at the frustrations you encountered upon Earth.

Look at what you did there, that wasn't a good thing was it? And all the while the little devil's assistant will sit on a little matt with a scorching melting pen and tick of all these numbers that will all fly up into the air like sparks into a fire and go back up this black chimney that spouts out and keeps the devils cottage warm, his little holiday home before he comes down to view the new residents of the black pit, and then you will really know what scoring points is. Hopefully the good deeds will be tallied up fair and balanced too and you may not dwell as long as you feared in the lower realms, yet it will not matter, as it's all the great cycle, the mistakes were not this life time's your own. Just the past that you must keep trying to better until eventually you reach the upper echelons of Heavens Nirvana.

My worst hangovers before I'd gotten on the almighty wagon, would see me for maybe a week at times move no more than you would see a house spider guest scurry around the edges of its preferred ceiling. My holidays were nothing more now than tired jaunts to the porcelain God to heave forth almighty projections of poisoned vomit. Even though I'd not touched a drop for two years the habit of retching up my entire guts seemed to remain, and if anything was getting worse. I guess the mixing of the oils to help cure the dreaded C was partly the cause too. The worst of these episodes of sickness though were when I felt I spotted the black dust again. It had happened on a grand scale on a visit to the hospital one time. An almighty bender had ended with me laid unconscious on these hard cobbles at the back of a rather grand looking corn exchange building in the great market town of Leeds. Jolly enough for many hours until I felt a shift in the atmosphere in this rough arse public house and that recollection in a hazy sense that when I had supped up to find another watering hole I had heard a thud of boots running behind me and then the feeling next of flying forward in the air and then nothing. I'd returned to the light rubbing the nasty gash in the back of my head, sticky mattered hair with splinters of glass. The focus returning some and me spotting a large rum bottle shattered near to me. It was not this that had seen me into the hospital though. I'd managed to get a train back to the station out in the sticks where I'd bought the house that I nick named debut. The little local pub down the lane from it had seen me stumble in looking rather worse for wear, yet I'd got the raging thirst for more pints of ale, the landlord mistaking my concussion for a more inebriated state than I was in. The smash around the head, apart from knocking me out for God only knows how long, had to be fair also sobered me right up. The argument in the local soon became heated and like all pubs in the corner, quietly sat this have a go hero, who taking offense to me picking up a fresh pint pot off the bar that was not mine and after taking a sip, sliding along the bar along with the beer to an almighty messy crash on the patterned carpet floor. I'd been more or less shown the door, with the landlords wife coming out after the scrum to whisper in my ear that my coat collar was thick with an unsightly amount of congealed blood and that she had called me a taxi with instructions to attend the A & E.

So it was here where I found myself, and where I first vomited the black dust, as the triage had taken one look at me and whizzed me straight through for emergency stitches to be put into the back of my head. They also found while checking my ribs for breakage a rather ugly black bruise on my spine the size of a large footed man. When I'd been seen and given a discharge note and a stern warning to not drink for a good period, I had wondered down the wrong corridors of the hospital looking to exit when I'd become very dizzy and nauseous. I'd side stepped into a bathroom and sank to my knees at the open lid and just in time too as a sudden explosion hit me from deep low in my guts. I expected projectile vomit as that's how it felt rising but it was more a freak out than just puke. A black dust sprayed from my mouth and covered the entire white porcelain system. The stark contrast of the clinical white and the black dust scared the hell out of me. I was slumped against the bottom of the toilet pan when a porter found me and called for a Dr to help me. The bruising from my spine must have caused internal bleeding, which upon crusting up had flown out of me like a fine mist of black dust. I'd not drunk for a week after that incident, yet even that had not been enough and I'd started screwing the caps off bottles of rum for medicinal purposes, or that's what I told my mind when any form of reason came to say STOP.

I think only weeks later my hand was put through some other pub window, which had seen wild jagged shards hit the green baize of the pool table and gone all into the pool team captains pint of John Smiths. It had been another boozer crossed of the ever growing list of barred establishments I had on record. I'd eventually begun drinking further on the outskirts of the city, grabbing my pints and sitting quiet in a corner dreaming out of the windows or staring down at my shoes willing myself to stop with the next round and head back home to my responsibilities as a husband. She had not left me when I was a public house man. No, it had only been after I had gained a murderous reputation for instability and continued my jollies now in the comfort of my own home that she had blown her final fuse.

My intentions had always set off good. I was quite the charmer when I wanted to play that role. Mixing her favourite cocktail and running candle lit baths after she waltzed through the door from work in the early years eager to see if I'd spent the day in a flurry of activity typing up my new great novel.

I had drawn the line when the wife had pulled out of the boot of the car one day, as I had been peeping around the thick tapestry curtain to see and scrutinize in some vain hope that she would delve in and bring back out of the dark boot confines into the summer air a light shining brown and dangerously gleaming bottle of my favourite liquid demon. But she never did dare to join me or even slightly encourage me, and I guess I could not really blame her. But when she pulled out a bumper pack of nappies that for me was a step too fuckin far, no matter how in tatters physically my manhood had become. I was not going to condemn myself to her suggestion of becoming some bloody newborn in the house I had bloody well paid for with my very mature thoughts, and if I shit or pissed upon the vast array of rugs and tiled to high heaven antique patterned carpets, then I bloody well would do.

To be totally honest it had by her been a rather good idea, as I was soiling myself through sheer loss of rational thought quite a number of times at my very worst. I'd even stopped hiding the fact, yet at that time of year I was still somehow pumping out rather large portions of text on the trusty old royal typewriter, but sly as ever I had started to hear her creeping about outside my office door and I had, when the drinking started to really interfere, tap with one hand on the keys, hitting any old button hfdhgfjgfunrfjhufbfudunjjiiujknj, a bit like that, while holding in my other hand the comfort of a full glass of my brown liquid demon.

I'd gone to kiss her goodnight one evening when I'd been guzzling from the neck of an open bottle of scotch. Her rebuff harsh as she had screamed at me to get away from her and that my breath stunk of piss.

Weeks later I'd gotten sudden diarrhea and found that instead of looking down the toilet pan at some resemblance of a late night curry, I had actually found the entire bog covered with my bright red blood. It looked like I'd cut the head off a live chicken and shaken its necks gaping wound all over the pan.

I'd naturally panicked, yet I'd told her zilch. After one full roll of paper hadn't cleaned me up I'd jumped in the shower and watched the blood run out of my arse and down my leg to swirl away down the plug, leaving me with a terrible premonition that my time was up.

I'd called an old friend, someone who had published my early work of short stories and poems before I'd hit the big time with my debut novel. He was married to a fantastic Dr who ran private clinics and who after a brief chat down the phone line had agreed to take some tests and get me scanned in an MRI machine to ascertain if I had a likely prognosis that didn't look like a death sentence. Three weeks of agonising worrying and waiting the reply came. I had cancer, mainly in the bowel and liver and lung. No more of the convo I heard but after the shock of it all wore off I recalled the other minor things mentioned. From the scan it looked like I had at best 6 months. Yet against all the odds I managed to keep it at bay and even when she finally slammed out of the marital homes door, I'd still held back from saying what I had, as I know it would have just been pity I was hoping for.

I'd found a cure in cannabis oil. An old farmer who I knew from way back sorted me out the right stuff to ingest, as one morning I had been sat out near the perimeter of my garden boundaries, close enough for him on his tractor to see me over the hedge and cut the engine for a bit of idle gossip. The sixty gram in ninety day method had seen me zonk right out and float around in the wee hours hypnotized and tripping with delight. It had even gotten the writing juices flowing again, or so I would think at the time, only to read back in the morning lights reality, not quite certain of my thoughts or rationale. But it put me in a good frame of mind to beat the dreaded C and it was compared to the poor sheep, swallowing the systems dreaded chemo, a piece of cake, and probably a damn sight more effective too.

I'd woken heavy as usual. The hangover not even there, yet its distinct flavours hung in the inside chambers of my head space. An alarm rages in the distance, a jack hammer being driven into the ground by some youthful energy, a car back firing constant, dogs howling and crows in nearby trees screeching, and its going into the very core of my brain receptors. The house is empty though, windows shut tight, and there is no real noise. It's all just a long playing nightmare memory that I wake to each day.

Like when I stupidly nearly tried the Doctors rigid approach to cancer treatments. I recall sitting in the sparse yet plush office of the oncologist while he shuffled through the door and spoke of his book knowledge on chemo being such a wonderful discovery. I'd been so scared and confused at that given moment in rime that I'd signed the forms, yes the one where the first side effect you read about is that you will have a major heart attack within the first years of the course, as it weakens the fuck out of your heart muscles. He had looked through his horn rimmed glasses and answered my inquiry as to just what it felt like being on such a cocktail of drugs.

"Well Sean let's say, take your worst hangover and times it by a thousand!" I'd laughed and spat the tepid water from the little white plastic cup I'd been sipping from all over my suited pants knee.

"Doc, do you know how fuckin bad I've had hangovers, a thousand times? You may as well kill me and seal me in the box right this instant, but tell my friends I want two gold sovereign coins placing on my eyes for the ferry man to get me over the river Styx, one dated on my year of birth and the other on the year we are in right now as I prepare to shake of this human vessel body and soar away in soul and spirit towards my rebirth day"

He had looked at me in a forlorn way, as if thinking maybe this cancer I'd caused all by myself after the dangerous lifestyle I'd lived for decades, and he was probably right.

Thankfully I'd not taken the stuff, my farmer friend giving me an alternative that meant the only poisoning to be done to me would be if I screwed the cap off a favourite bottle myself.

I'd remember back to before she had left me. A long way back I had to go, to recall the days where we would fall out of bed after making sweaty beautiful love and just grab a leisurely cup of mint tea and pull on scruffs of clothes and head out the back gate into the wonderful bright early dawn of the countryside waking up. Where after walking a mile or two we would just embrace, pulling our bodies close into each other and feel the sun warm our faces as we closed our eyes and I sniffed her hair of rose petals fragrance.

All long gone, replaced by the rancid smell off standing by the decaying pool side and sniffing the gut rut swirling down below.

I was on the edge of the pool side again. Looking down I'd counted around fifty bottles smashed and scattered down there in the confines of where a normal person would have aqua blue water to dive into. Not this murky brown liquid with its soggy labels and sharp angry spikes of glass. I was impressed with my will power to be doing this smashing feat of restraint, as in my early drinking years, when I knew the grip of addiction was tighter than a Houdini knot, there were more likely to be five hundred bottles smashed up, yet the pool was filling nicely from the five hundred plus bottles where I'd managed in the first year of being alone to pour in, loosing complete sight of the tiled floor.

I would wade in for a paddle shoeless, careful with my balance down the stairs, weaving around obvious sticking up shards of broken bottle pieces that had scattered up this end, after throwing them in from the edge of the deep.

My bandaged feet unravelling as I'd not bothered dressing any fresh shard cut wounds for months now, as a smell of rotting made me think maybe gangrene had set in .

I think seriously I was already drown n dead here, or at least in my mind, visioning myself as a human before I stepped off, my soul now the sole controller of what would be seen and heard and viewed. It was not a relief though as besides the memories of my addiction sadly whizzing through my last time and space I also had a much softer whispering voice telling me that we can only look and think a little while longer Sean, as it is time for your new body. The new body part kind of filled me with an exhilaration yet it could be any body, an annoying blood sucking mosquito, or one of those unlucky bumble bees that panic and sting when there was really no danger, leaving me without my stinger and another rebirth to contemplate as I'd had no time to make progress.

I had a strong feeling I was coming back human though. To really be put to the test again on this watery planet. The flashbacks you have with Dejavu are all past lives, which is why they are so dreamy yet so damn sure that you have been n seen before that scene or phrase.

One minute the soul would be me on the other side of the pool watching myself recall my past life and its failures and the next I'd be stepping off and start to swirl around the brown watery liquid of the whiskey pool and the next I'd get flashes again, filled with serene panic as I was back in the throes of death, tumbling down to the waters deep dark recesses, gasping for air yet enjoying in a perverse addicted way that the lungs were filling to over capacity with my favourite brown liquid.

Thankfully I'd thrown away my guns the Christmas holidays just passed. The last act after loading the Luper pistol and stuffing it as far into my mouth as I could manage without gagging all over the metal cylinders

Id thrown others in the dark oily pools of water that now laid at the bottom of barge canal locks. I had enough still about me to not want to end it in a bloody mess. No, I wanted to swim into my rebirth, or at least feel the liquid around my dying figure as I passed on through.

I woke with a start as sudden as if my heart had frozen upon waking. A terrible nightmare had brought me out of my deep sleep as its realism became enough to convince me to run. The scene had been one of me being held down while a small group of masked figures took it in turns to brand my naked skin on my upper body and inner thighs with painful pressured scolds. I could see large pins penetrating into this bubble like existence which I felt was my new soul.

Vivid dreams mixed inside these nightmares.

Lighting incense in Penang in the temples of George towns little India district, climbing the hill to the freedom fighters fort in India's Arambol district, as Tiracol fort, the last stance of the indian man before the Portuguese kidnapped the country for over four hundred years loomed large and serene upon the cliff tops. I'd let the monks serve me oolong tea and chanted mantras alongside their thousand year old frames.

I'd meditated in the oil dark nights of Arabian deserts in Abu Dhabi in the United Arab Emirates before the tourists came.

It was like the beach house my oldest friend owned before he died of an ALCOHOL OVERDOSE, where he lived in on the beaches of North Goa. The cave house was hard to explain sufficiently on paper as you came out from smoking Tola the size of pizza to the white sands.

My other black friend who owned a back yard that stretched for miles full of cannabis plants swaying like drunken revellers, just a ten minute stroll away too.

Mexico temples and underwater caves of fresh pool waters that I'd spiritualised myself in

All youthful endeavours that I felt my dreams were trying to help pull me through the nightmares of a late, the travel easy back then with bundles of plentiful cash from the book sales.

I guess I could have been tested for my drug intake over the early years of my life, yet I doubted I would be re-birthed as a crying screaming heroin baby, rattling alone on the secure ward for infants born in this cruel way. No, my test would involve the grog again I was so sure of that fact. It was needed, the new test. I hoped deep in my heart that I would find the courage this time to kick the habit of alcoholism and let my rebirth after that life be a good enough one, so as to pass on from the wheel of life and taste the pleasure that awaits in Nirvana.

All these dreams and nightmares mingling inside my head space, confusing me totally as to what was real anymore. As my eyes remained closed shut on the edge of the pool side, I'd open them with dizzying dread and stare down disorientated into the brown liquid of my rebirth. The only times I were sure I wasn't quite dead yet was when the pains in my liver ached so bad it was like constant torture on specific areas, by well-trained military men specially adapt and hardened in breaking a human soul.

The inevitable plunge came, yet most unexpected as I'd have to say I'd not had a bad morning, with only an ebb of energy vanishing in the afternoon. So when the plunge into the deep end happened, it not only woke me when time had finally run out but it gave me an almighty sense of what if, like one of my favourite quotes from the beat master Kerouac,' What's in store for me in the direction I don't take?'

Life and its full circle philosophy became my true sense of purpose. Born at two minutes to midnight and by the pool clock which by some miracle still worked when everything else around the house seemed doomed to break, it had read back to me that it was five minutes to the witching hour of a new day. The few minutes before I'd stepped off the cool broken mosaic tiles that I'd had shipped in from morocco when back in the day there seemed a purpose to laying beauty around the home, before she left me to suffer in my own silence, it must have been more or less the same time for birth as my now fresh departure into my death..

Like the slippery canal of birth I fell now in reverse towards the icy dark spirit laden liquid of rebirth.

In my youth I'd studied in India before returning to Europe and meeting my future wife in the port of Stavanger in Norway. I'd indoctrinated my-self enough with the theories to believe and know at the shambolic end of what I'd failed miserably to uphold on any Buddhist levels, that I would and rightly so be returning on this sacred wheel of life to try again, and to put into practice the mistakes of this miserable attempt at enlightenment.

I would no doubt return as another wretch of a creature. A TEST to see if I would continue to spin on this axle of failure or if by some hard won and belligerent miracle become at peace in the garden of nirvana. HA HA, not a chance my old dear boy, echoes around the pool house walls.

I had the drowning first though. The gash that luckily knocked me unconscious as I hit head first through the shards of all my bottles of un drunken misery, a few more jagged shards catching my neck veins and bleeding me profusely as I swirled around in the confusion of that moment.

I was destined to see the fall. Previously warned by standing on the edge way too many times of just what awaited me if I ever fell right off and entered the whiskey pool. The unconsciousness probably a last act of kindness from God as he too must have been sick and tired of watching me struggle with the dark pains. Spurts of bright blood and stinging in my neck my last sights on this ocean heavy planet, as the rebirth had surely begun, though what fate awaits a man who fails, and how many rebirths was this now?

It was not the death I had envisioned as a young man on the verge of commercial success. My debut novel and its follow up had gained quite the momentum in the market to keep the till registers ringing and the publishers fat pockets even more bulbous. The third had seen an almighty decline in my popularity due to an unfortunate libel case that I had fought with the best of lawyers but still came away with a loss of victory that had more or less swallowed what funds I had left on the cases court costs. It had been around the same year when I had gone from feelings of grandeur, enough to seriously enquire about a burial plot in the poets corner of Pierre le chaise to realising that no grand spot for my broken useless bones would befit such an area of buried talent and that I would end up like the poor wretches of the world on the scrap heap of a mass shared commercial bone yard. Although to be fair the cemetery had lost some of its unique edge over the years, as you couldn't go and squat besides Morrison's bust no longer in the candle lit night nor could you climb on to the top of the huge trumpeted angel Sphinx flying majestic over Wilde's tomb to read his epitaph from his work, A ballad of reading gaol,

[And Alien tears will fill for him

Pity's long-broken urn,

For his mourners will be outcast men,

And outcasts always mourn.]

The giddy Parisian girls smudging bright lipstick all over the face of the angel had seen a hideous plastic box of Perspex erected around Oscars resting place which he would have found rather crude and hated, just as Jim would have come out drunkenly swinging and spoiling for a fight as the lizard king took offence to the guards that now stood sentry rigid either side of his spot in the poets corner. His bust long gone as again the Paris urchins firstly stealing his nose until the tomb keepers placed it into storage for safe keeping.

With the little mound of coins I had left rotting in the bank vaults I had booked a flight to the states and gone on some weird pilgrimage to follow my writing hero's like Kerouac and Burroughs. I had already three years before, flush on the success of the crime debut taking the charts by storm, travelled the emerald isles retracing the Behan brogues in drink n political song. A small part of memory tumbling forth a verse now as I sang much quieter these days to no one but the wall,

'T'was beyond at Mick Reddins, at Owen Doyle's wedding, the lads got the pair of us for a reel,

Says I, "Boys, excuse us," says they, "don't refuse us,"

"I'll play nice and aisy," said Larry O'Neill.

Then up we got leppin' it, kickin' and steppin' it,

Herself and myself on the back of the door,

Till Molly, God bless her, fell into the dresser,

And I tumbled over a child on the floor.

The America trip though had turned out a disaster, as I'd fell quite ill in St Louis and after travelling in the style of my favourite dharma bums down into Mexico searching for Burroughs's famous Yage plant. I should have taken heed of William S debut junky though, as he had warned upon the terrible predicament I found myself in at the very end of my life. Maybe I would have turned out so much for the better if I'd continued on my voyage of discovery through the wonders of drugs that help the mind see and feel the true concepts to life and its after living realms.

No the booze had been the biggest curse I'd ever gotten my wretched mind involved with, as the Government the biggest cruel demon sellers out there, flashed neon bar signs at me, pulling my drunken frame into the doors of intoxication hovels. Seven eleven stores were just as bad as they gave me that early withdrawing availability on tap, as I'd been able to get my grubby hands at any time on the demon brown liquid that whiskey had become.

The morphine and heroin of my youth should have been what sustained me throughout and more than likely stopped the inevitable plunge of my drunken foolish death.

In the delta state is not where I have lived out my nocturnal revitalising. My piss poor sporadic cycles of sleep at best had been underwhelming. Towards the end, when I had returned home I had struggled increasingly at the edge of the pool's dangerous lip, and only by the grace of God not tumbling spectacularly in did I sleep for an hour at most. Those waking moments of worry, where the antique swords and daggers purchased over the years now stood for some feeble protection against God only knows what was lurking in my anxiety propelled visions and dreams. Again they were nothing but stark reminders of how much I'd diverted off the noble path. My arc Angel Gabriel rubbing out my forehead mark as I slumbered in sleep, yet that mark I was never truly sure upon receiving in the first place, as my life had become dismal. The other marking had been put upon me, as the tormentors seemingly had their way with my life and soul for as long as I could remember. I hoped and knew deep down that this time I'd be reborn and marked with the R by Gabriel, for I was sure about one thing more than any other about rebirth, that no matter what you came back as , be it human form or animal or a piece of stone in a mountain majestic setting, looking down royally on fields powdered by natures array of wild colour flowers, you would always be born into the same star sign, the same era of time, so I knew within my dying heart I would always remain an age of Aquarian, and that it had not been a failure on my guardian angels part to heal me and protect me, for it had all laid at my feet, as I'd ignored the signs to tune into my powerful assets gifted by the Gods and suffered like a fool for my ignorance.

It was a little like the clocks when I looked after waking, and they would all be stuck on the same time all around the house as if some ghoul in the spirit world had demanded they all be silent n still. This had gone on for months where every time I dared look at a clock face it was stuck on exactly the same time, which happened to be two minutes to twelve. I trod the squeaky floorboards of the house. Years ago the annoyance had been great within me, as spending all that money on pure carved wood, yet now in my drunken abstinence they comforted me as if I was upon the swelled ocean in my own tiny vessel, just secure in the design of not sinking, the creak reassuring that I was not alone, at least not entirely.

'Let him become a fool that he may become wise', the saying that I'd read from Kerouac searching his bible after hitching through the winter to spend Christmas with his mother in his story, the dharma bums became a fitting mantra as I rocked on my tip toes back n forth against the drop edge of the pool side. I knew I'd screwed the bottle top off this time, the fire running down my throat as I let the air, that last living gasp of air sail from my mouth, the liquid now pounding in the swirl of my fall into the pool. The giant top had come off now, soon enough my life ebbed away in a moment of panic and then calm.

Nothing to really fear, Death just another dimension, like some clinical waiting room before a power being beyond human mortal comprehension summons you for the last time by your birth name on earth and gives you the instructions briefly about your new direction for your soul and then before you know it the rebirth is well and truly upon you.

I had been correct about the rebirth into human form, an infant birth I recalled now as I stood gazing out of a large stone opening, one which looked out past large wooden shutters as my gaze fell across the thousands of acres of vine yards stretching out before my sight in the Spanish sunshine. Reborn as a youthful young man, I could feel the memories of my new birth, yet I couldn't grasp for the life in me anything in-between the time of that deliverance and now, some fifteen years later, except for two over powering fascinations with writing quaint stories that were always seemingly powered by an unknown force of regurgitated memory, and the second of my personal meditations that drew strength from the Buddhist philosophies upon life and death.

I'd recall as my schooling nearly at an end, my father so proud yet baffled about my significant body of literature that I was producing. I knew it was the man I had been in previous lifetime, the writer who had failed and had yet tried I felt, to better himself in some portion of his time on earth.

I was wise for my years, keen upon all things spiritual, especially the Buddhist approach to life. I woke to rituals that I felt were strongly imbedded into my DNA fabric, my readings upon rebirth from the Buddhist texts my father sourced for me as he had seen my keen determined ways to enlighten my young mind, were no doubt the thoughts and remembering that I felt. Who had I been? Who had he been before? The road long and winding and vast as an ocean bed was deep. Was infinity my old self, cave men, aliens, bugs, a simple drop of water in a stream, which then for years rode me out in my DNA fabric as a river, as a vast deep lake, as the ocean itself, did I then become animal, the lowest form in the seas or did I evolve all the way through until majestic as a whale? Is that the point you reach to then become human? Our human fascination with the oceans maybe a deeper rooted idea, more than just curiosity and more a revisit to places we had lived out many lives before.

Yet for all my serenity and peace, I felt a powerful urge towards the vast fields where rows upon rows for miles laid wine berries like in the Grapes of wrath, awaiting my plucking fingers, as the those workers filling huge baskets with grapes as big as fresh blooming Rose buds, and noisy tractors pulling away carts brimming and overflowing with the crops. The operation huge and something my Father had developed from his line of parents and there's, stretching back hundreds of years into the Diablo wine family.

He wanted me a scholar though, relieved when I had shown such fortitude with my early studies, proud of my spiritual endeavours at such a tender age. Yet in my quiet time alone, the pull was there to ruin it all. Somewhere deep within I would flash thoughts of swimming naked with a secret lover in the huge vats that swirled our family product. To lie in the fields until burnt by the midday Spanish sun and be fed like an

Emperor by my workers, feeding me with stems rammed with luscious grapes plump with intoxicating juices. It was a shocking feeling to have this reckless vein of thought running through my mostly serene mind.

It came in dreams of pure abandonment of my responsibilities. The problem being that as I speak of my father he is passed away now quite some time. A problem of the liver that he had kept secret from me until there was no time to summon even the best Drs in Europe to consult on a saving procedure.

Id turned the correct age to inheriton the day I had gone with my family solicitor to a small court in the town, to be read the will that I knew the contents of anyway. Father over these years would always lead me around on horseback together, bordering our entire estate and proudly opening his arms as we rode, say, "Son this will all be your land one day, keep my name alive," then roaring with hard laughter shouting back at me as he galloped away, "don't be drinking all the profits."

Back home the mood sombre from the skeleton staff that I'd allowed to work while the will reading took place. I wasn't sad though for my father, as he had lived a full life his own way and what more could man do. I alone knew the answer as I headed out on my majestic horse **DE GOZO** at a steady gallop, until a mile away I reached the wide streams that fed out into the Spanish coast line seas.

Dismounted, I ventured towards my favourite meditation spot on the banking, near to a small yet forceful waterfall that cascaded down to the right of where I know sat in the lotus position. The bubbles as they filled with oxygenised energy, newly formed from the falls powerful cascade were young souls, as rebirth, as quick at times as a bursting bubble upon a river side became my serene thoughts. Hundreds gathered and burst forth again into new rebirthed lives. Maybe a continued conveyer belt of forming as a water surface bubble, only to burst and reappear again as another, your popping delayed by a further moment, one that teaches from the view of the above water gods. You eventually get downstream, as in life, you blew candles in honour of your time lengthening.

A new more powerful thought over took my mind as I seemingly day dreamed into a scene as real as the day's sun shining down upon my warming head.

I was stood outside a shack, nestled into the side of a roaring beach side, where the spray from the rolling waves was finding my face as we were that close to the shore. I wandered without hesitation towards the sanded down three tier steps that led upwards to a wrapped around veranda, my hand large in my vision as I push steadily open the door and enter.

Inside the room I find emptiness, except I notice a shelf of books in a neat row, yet the titles were unseen as the books were placed so the page edges were facing outwards and not the spines, where the titles would be easily read. The two book ends holding the collection steady were one full bottle of whiskey, yet the other side had upon it an emptied bottle, with a note in a scroll rolled up inside.

There was a back door ajar to the property which I exited out of into a winding sand path, which started its swerving at the bottom of identical steps as the front.

I started meandering down the path, taking in the scents of the large lavender bushes that were well established to the front border of the path, a back drop behind of high stemmed red hot poker plants, giving a vibrant contrast to the scene.

I snaked around the path and left the sounds more distant of the front heaving ocean and travelled on until I came upon a large still clear lake. The only things upon its shore line were a small wooden row boat with some red oars lent up against its hull, while a man dressed like he had washed ashore from some shipwreck, remained still with his back to me, gazing out at something that he only knew of its importance.

I set the boat out into the lake and pushed off with the oars and steadily stroked the water with the poles until I gathered momentum to leave the rowing and sit back and enjoy staring over the side, into what revealed itself to be an array of different coloured crystals like, Tigers eye, which I knew was for seeking clarity, there were Lapis Lazuli, which helped in expanding ones awareness, while the Rose Quartz calmed me as the boat bobbed about on gentle lapping waves of love glistening in the suns reflected shine.

Upon reaching the other shore which had only been a small distance away, I left the boat upon the grass verge and found myself at the foot of a winding path that led off upwards in quite a rise. The wooded shaded path continued to rise as I made good progress, with my mind wondering where it led. Around half way up I heard a rustling of something large coming towards me from the left hand side. To my amazement out strolled as casual as you like, a magnificent black silk furred panther. I stood froze to the spot wondering if this was where I woke from my meditative state, just as I the devoured became. Yet the animal padded stealthily towards me and nuzzled into my leg with its huge head.

I felt no fear, and stroked the beast with my hands, even tickling its ears, until it turned and darted off with a powerful lunge back from where it had firstly appeared from.

I continued upward on the winding path until eventually I arrived at the top which spread out into an oval flat setting of crushed stones that in the sunlight looked like shards of glass for a floor.

I looked around for the significance of what I felt surely was something for me to find, yet I viewed nothing, except a clear horizon.

I waited a while, no more than five minutes for a sign and then turned and made the journey back more or less the same as I had on my arrival. The only difference this time was that the panther didn't show from the dense foliage, yet at the spot we had met he gave a loud roar to let me know he was close and watching out for me.

Back at the wooden hut, I climbed the back stairs and entered the square empty room again. The only change to the viewed scene was the bottles had now both changed places, from one end of the books row to the other, and the first book in the row had been turned to reveal its title running down its spine, giving a vital clue to the ink that lay waiting to be read inside its pages.

At this point I blinked my eyes and felt the sun burn back into my pupil as I looked at the view back sat at my spot near the waterfall. I noticed first under close inspection of my fingernail, the whole spectrum of colours in the entire palette of the Universe.

I closed my eyes again into my meditation by the waterfall and finally turned off the powerful forces sound. I knew it was there, as I knew only too well the pull of past addictions were there too, set deep into my infrastructure as the man I had been many, many times upon this Planet, yet I felt this time I wouldn't drink the worries my Father had jokingly warned me about when it came to my vast inherited estate, as the lives lived on the edge disappeared like fine sand through my open hands. I needed no senses now, enlightened, I had finally arrived...

This book is dedicated to all the liquid addicts, God bless your souls.

And to all the Dharma bums, keep chanting, for we know it eventually ends in bliss.

DBH. September 2018.

Also available from Dale Brendan Hyde

THE INK RUN

A NOVEL VIGILANTE

OTISS is an abused child, physically & mentally tortured for years in the home by his sadistic parents. His Father STAN plots an elaborate alibi enabling him to set up the boy for the murder of his own Mother.

A trial of sorts, hanging on the basis of a defense of automatism (murder when sleepwalking) sees a detainment to the FABERON institution for the criminal insane.

In this cloudy pond, where the staff are every bit as dangerous & disturbed as the patients.

Young OTISS is placed on a wing funded as a trial by the Government which uses olden day methods from centuries past to cure madness.

Eventually released a decade later as an even more tortured soul, he sets up THE VILLAGE EYE pub as a front to his real nocturnal activities of being a VIGILANTE.

Warning beatings on the scum of the village soon becomes tiresome as he reaches new limits of retribution.

Still traumatized from youth, will he find the courage to finally confront STAN?

You can't truly escape your blood lines DNA as fatal mistakes see a familiar face from the INSTITUTION reveal that our main protagonist has not been the only one keeping the VIGIL & upping the ANTE.

Also available from Dale Brendan Hyde

THE GODS 'R' WATCHIN

A COLLECTION OF POETRY FIRSTLY PUBLISHED SO AS TO
STIPULATE THE ENTRY REQUIREMENTS FOR THE TS
ELLIOT PRIZE FOR BEST NEW VERSE. NOW SOME TWENTY
YEARS LATER IT HAS BEEN REVISED AND UPDATED TO
INCLUDE FURTHER FRESH POEMS. IT IS FOR SALE TO THE
GENERAL PUBLIC FOR THE VERY FIRST TIME.

Coming soon from Dale Brendan Hyde

THE DICE

WITH ONE FATAL ROLL, IT COULD BE YOU!

Four serial killers busy doing what they do best. Although one is now dead as a coffin nail. Executed & fried good by old sparky for his heinous crime spree that totalled out at fourteen victims.

Two more are active in the general Texas area, yet the police don't even have them on their radar. The body count is rapidly rising.

Then across the Atlantic pond is the fourth. Where a stop start investigation has come to a halt. Baffled, the Greater Manchester police can't decide if the mysterious pusher case is for real. Yet more bodies keep floating up from the canal areas and to one detective he's convinced that a serial killer is roaming the darkened towpaths looking for fresh victims.

In amongst all this mayhem is widower Shail Singleton. Ten years now she has lived in small town dripping springs, Texas. After fleeing her beloved Ireland with the still raw memory of her husband murdered on their own doorstep.

She only has one good trusted friend in this new town. Old Walter runs the local thrift shop and he understands her fears & dreams. Unbeknown to Shail though, all these lives are inextricably linked. And they are hurtling to a murderous conclusion, for even the executed leave things behind.

Coming soon from Dale Brendan Hyde

STITCHED

A MISCARRIAGE OF JUSTICE INQUIRY

ONCE YOU'RE DEAD

THE TRUTH BECOMES SO MUCH CLEARER